melanie walsh

my beak,
your beak

Picture Corgi

Sausage dogs
are long with
little legs.

Dalmatians are tall
and spotty. But...

they both love
chasing sticks!

grrrr

Sharks swim in the deep ocean.

Goldfish swim
in a bowl.
But...

pip!

they both
blow bubbles!

Penguins live in
the snowy South Pole.

Robins live in the garden. But...

they both have
pointy beaks!

yum

Lions are big and have hairy manes.

Kittens are small
and fluffy.

But...

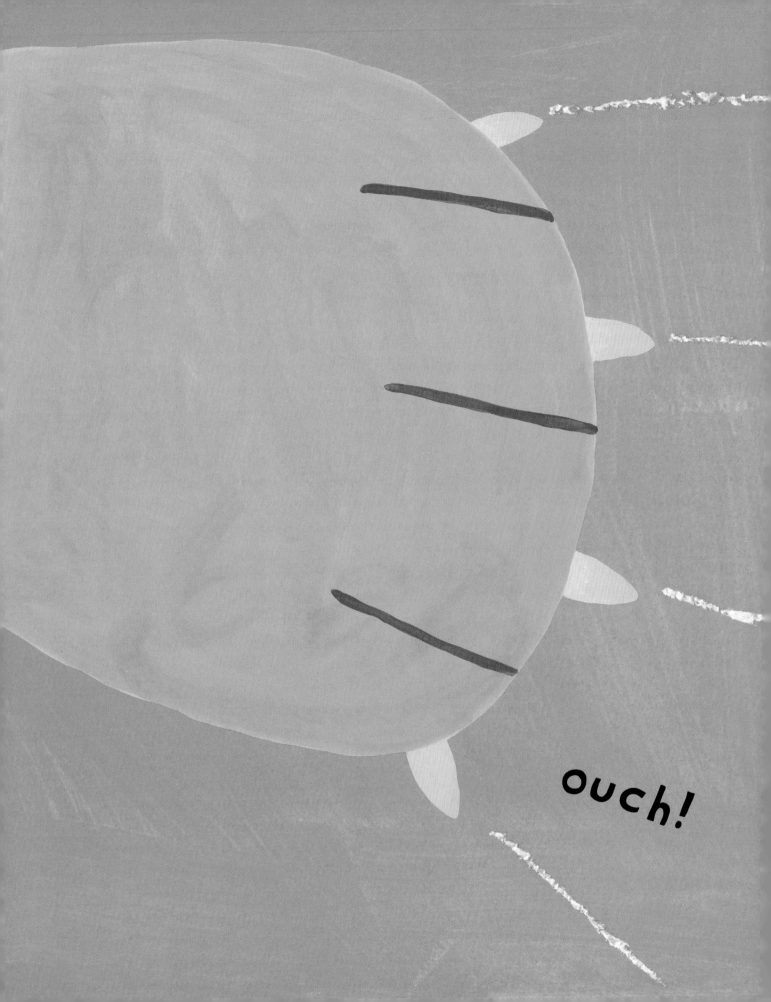

ouch!

they both have
scratchy claws!

Bush-babies sleep
in trees.

Bats sleep in
dark caves.
But...

they're both
wide awake at night!

goodnight!

MY BEAK, YOUR BEAK
A PICTURE CORGI BOOK 0 552 547654

First published in Great Britain by Doubleday,
an imprint of Random House Children's Books

Doubleday edition published 2002
Picture Corgi edition published 2003

1 3 5 7 9 10 8 6 4 2

Copyright © Melanie Walsh, 2002

The right of Melanie Walsh to be identified as the author of this work has been
asserted in accordance with the Copyright, Designs and Patents Act 1988.

Picture Corgi Books are published by Random House Children's Books,
61-63 Uxbridge Road, London W5 5SA, a division of The Random
House Group Ltd. London, Sydney, Auckland, Johannesburg

THE RANDOM HOUSE GROUP Limited Reg. No. 954009
www.kidsatrandomhouse.co.uk

A CIP catalogue record for this book is available
from the British Library.

Printed in Singapore